Christmas Tea Cakes

By Carolena DeMille

$\mathcal{M}$y life began on Christmas Day in 1943 at 3:35 p.m. est. As I drew my first breath, the nurses chimed "Mary" and the women doctor followed with "Carol". So, since Mary Carol was very appropriate for a Christmas baby, it became my name.

My Dad was a lieutenant fighting on the Pacific Front near the Philippines on the day I was born. We did not meet until I was two years old. Fortunately my mom had her parents, four sisters and one brother to help her until he returned home.

Since Dad was a thirty year professional Army officer, we celebrated many Christmases in some of the most beautiful places in the world. I remember how elated I was when the snow began falling and covering the wintry landscapes of some places we called home like Germany, Alaska, and Switzerland.

My favorite setting was in Switzerland. It is a kindred spirit for me. My great grandfather (Rudolph Johann) came from a little town called Aarau near Zurich. He was a Master carpenter in his country. One of the stories I was told about him was when he came to the United states in the late 1800's, He took a job at a high school in Ohio as a carpenter. He always wore his traditional black, broad brimmed, carpenter's hat. The kids soon started to call him "Caps" so Caps became his nickname from then on.

I have to mention a little tidbit of information that I thought was interesting. The famous Albert Einstein finished high school in Aarau, Switzerland. A few years later, he became a Swiss citizen. I could go on but that is another story for later.

Christmas has always been such a huge part of my history and life, and after revealing a little bit of my history, my story centers around Germany. We always had amazing magical Christmases there. We were never disappointed. I remember the incredible smell of the new fallen snow, the crunch it made under my boots and just the beauty of the snow falling so silently. The many Christmas traditions and customs of Germany were experienced through the whole month of December. It was like living in a winter wonderland.

My family lived in a German neighborhood. My two best friends, Pam and Judy lived within a three block radius of my house. We were all ten years old or close to it.

Pam's parents hired a housekeeper from Russia named Laura. My favorite thing about Laura was that she always made sure that a beautiful large cut crystal cookie jar was full of walnut sized powered sugar cookies around the Christmas holidays. We would all run hungrily to Pam's house after school, and Laura would have milk and those delightful cookies ready for us to dive into. One weekend Judy and I were invited around Christmas time over to Pam's house for a sleep over. I always enjoyed their housekeeper named Natasha from Poland. She was all the time telling us Polish folklore stories.

While we were enjoying one of her stories, Laura popped in and asked if we would like some hot chocolate. Of course, who is going to refuse that? I jumped up and followed her to the kitchen to help and took the opportunity to ask her if she would teach me how to make her marvelous cookies. "Of course I will. In fact, I need to make some tonight" she said.

After we all enjoyed our delicious German hot chocolate drinks, I let everyone know that I was going to help Laura make some cookies for a late night snack. I was so excited and headed for the kitchen. It was a beautiful white and tan kitchen. There were large arch-shaped windows and more than ample pretty, blue cabinets. A huge butcher block counter, where Laura did all of her baking was in the center of the room. Already set-up were containers of fresh flour, powdered sugar, and jars of pecan halves. Beside the jars, stood a block of fresh butter and bottles of pure vanilla.

Laura said, "You must *always* use the finest and freshest ingredients." Paying very strict attention to her every move, I watched as she started adding the following ingredients into a big bowl:

1 cup butter (must use real butter!)

1/2 cup powdered sugar

1 1/2 cups flour

2 teaspoons pure vanilla

1 cup pecan halves, another chopped or 12 ounce bag of chopped pecans. Pecans are the only nut that helps to create the tantalizing, delicious aroma of these special cookies.

Laura mixed the ingredients in the order given. Once they were all mixed together well, she left the dough in the bowl, and put it in the refrigerator. Laura said, "The dough must be somewhat hard to form the balls."

This cookie can be made in two ways:

1. You can take a piece of dough and wrap it around one pecan half. Roll it into a ball about the size of a walnut and place on a cookie sheet.

2. You can add chopped pecans to the dough as you mix the ingredients.

Use a melon scooper to help shape the chilled dough into walnut size cookies. Place on a cookie sheet with a small space between cookies since they don't spread out much. Usually four cookies can be placed across on a 12" x 14" cookie sheet and as many down as the cookie sheet will allow

Try to use a stainless steel cookie sheet. Use the wrapper from the butter and rub it over the cookie sheet to apply on a small amount of coating. Over the years, I have practiced the habit of stacking the butter wrappers flat in my freezer to use when I bake.

Laura continued by saying, "Once the cookie sheet is full, place in an oven preheated to 400 degrees for 10 to 12 minutes. When removed from the oven, let them cool for about ten minutes because they are hot and have a tendency to crumble when hot." (I always liked my cookies a little brown on the bottom which takes 1 or 2 minutes longer.)

Laura added, "Place cookies on a plate. Sift powdered sugar into a big deep bowl. Add a couple cookies at a time to cover with the powdered sugar. Roll them around until they have a good layer covering them. Place cookies in a glass cookie jar with a lid. Right before serving, roll one more time in sifted powdered sugar to refresh. Never store or wrap in tin foil because cookies will absorb a metallic taste. Waxed paper or parchment paper is the best, and also, can be used to line a metal tin Christmas box."

We baked and baked those special cookies all evening. The air was saturated with the smell of butter and pecans. I felt awestruck that I was learning how to bake these "heavenly cookies" that I loved so much.

"What do you call these cookies Laura?" I asked.

"Russian Tea Cakes," Laura said.

"I will call them "Christmas Tea Cakes", I said. Is that okay?" Laura smiled and gave me a big hug. "That is perfectly fine," she said.

"Let's ask the others if they want to join us for some more hot chocolate and Tea Cakes." said Laura. In the cozy living room, we ate the heavenly Tea Cakes and enjoyed our hot chocolate while Natasha told us Christmas stories. We cuddled by the warm, crackling fire, and enjoyed the gorgeously decorated fir Christmas tree twinkling while we listened. Pam chimed in that my Birthday was coming up on Christmas day.

Natasha added, "You are very blessed."

"Why?" we all chimed in together.

Because, it is said in Polish folklore that anyone born on Christmas day is blessed with a free ticket to Heaven.

"Wow," we all said at once.

Natasha added, I wasn't born on Christmas day, but the name Natasha means...Christmas child, born on Christmas day.

"How amazing is that?" I said.

We all felt a special connection that Christmas.

I decided at that unusual moment, that my Christmas Tea Cakes would be baked at Christmas time only. Since the age of ten, I have made these unique cookies every Christmas throughout the years. People have begged me to make the "Tea Cakes" and asked for the recipe countless times. I have actually shared the recipe over the years with numerous people.

Now, I would like to share the recipe as my gift with anyone who wants to take the time to enjoy them too. The Tea Cakes are so easy to make, and bring so much pleasure. I do want to caution you that the Tea Cakes are addicting. You will find yourself craving them in the middle of the night. Your family with be begging you every day to bake them. Since they are so easy to make, you will be equally tempted. Seeing as I'm giving my favorite recipe as a gift, it will always be eagerly available and waiting for you in my book. My lifelong dream has been to write a special Christmas story that would hopefully become part of many people's Christmas traditions for many years to come. One day I realized that this wonderful recipe that I have treasured and baked every Christmas for so many years would be a great gift to give to the world as my Christmas story. I hope that this recipe will be a part of many people's Christmases for a long, long time like mine.

My next Christmas will be December 25, 2017. That will be my 74th Birthday and the 64th year that I will be baking and now sharing my Christmas Tea Cakes recipe and tradition. It will be the first year that I will be with anticipation, sharing them with the world.

Merry Christmas to all of you!

Always remember to leave a few Tea Cakes for Santa Claus. They are HIS favorite on Christmas Eve!

Print information available on the last page.

Rev. date: 05/24/2017

To order additional copies of this book, contact:
Xlibris
1-888-795-4274
www.Xlibris.com
Orders@Xlibris.com

Printed in the United States
by Baker & Taylor Publisher Services